Rebekah Wagner

Visiting HEAVEN

Visiting Heaven
This book is written to provide information and motivation to readers. Its purpose is not to render any type of psychological, legal, or professional advice of any kind. The content is the sole opinion and expression of the author, and not necessarily that of the publisher.

Printed in the United States of America.

ISBN 978-1-951913-96-0 (Paperback)
ISBN 978-1-951913-97-7 (Digital)

Lettra Press books may be ordered through booksellers or by contacting:

Lettra Press LLC
30 N Gould St. Suite 4753
Sheridan, WY 82801, USA
1 307-200-3414 | info@lettrapress.com
www.lettrapress.com

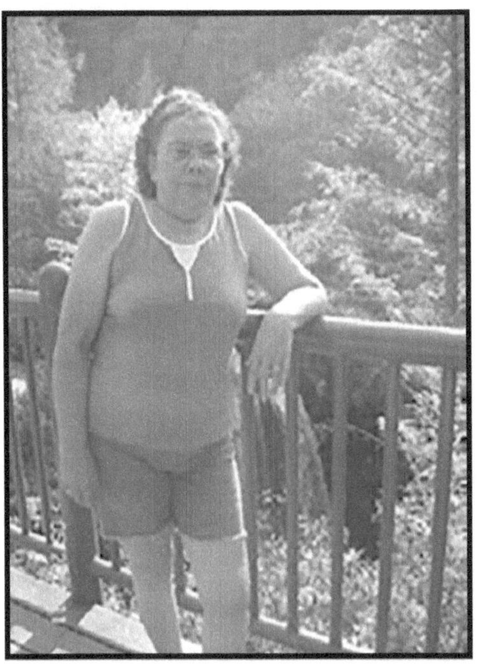

This book is in memory of my nanny
whom I miss dearly every day.

Just like to Tori my nanny was not just my grandmother,
she was my best friend. To many people she was not just
a mother, grandmother, sister, aunt or cousin she was a
person that you could talk to at any time about anything.
She would have coffee on in minutes and food at the
table if you wanted or needed it. She was always in a good
mood and ready to give or receive a good laugh.

As Always Nanny,
I love you up to the moon.

Chapter 1

As I hit the county line and was less than a mile away from my mom's I felt an excruciating pain in my chest and I knew she was gone.

When I reached the house, mom was waiting outside for me in the driveway.

"Tori don't go in there, she's gone baby. Just remember her the way she was before she got sick honey."

My mom said.

I stood in my mom's driveway sobbing because my best friend, my grandmother, my nanny was gone. She was no longer suffering, but I was angry and mad. The COPD had taken away the most important person in my life. I wanted to scream and kick like a kid throwing a tantrum, but I knew it wouldn't bring her back so I just fell to the ground quietly sobbing. How was I going to keep my promise to take care of myself? How was I going to live my life if the person that was always there when I needed her was gone?

As I watched the hearse take her away, I could feel myself slipping into a dark place that I had no idea how to get out of. If only I had gotten the chance to say goodbye, but I didn't, instead I got here too late. And now she was gone forever and there was nothing I could do about it.

The next couple of days were some of the hardest days that I had ever had to deal with. People came to pay their respects and honestly, it made me sick because hardly any of them came around when she was alive. What should have been a time that brought everyone together made me want to distance myself from everyone and everything.

Three Weeks Later

It had been three weeks since my nanny passed away and I hadn't offered to change clothes, go to work, shower, nothing. I was having a hard time grieving due to anger and the fact that I felt completely alone.

I had no idea what to do about it. I distanced myself from my mom and the rest of my so-called family was nowhere around. I was a complete mess. I was about to crawl back into bed when I heard a knock on my door. I opened the door to find my boss standing on my porch and he didn't look happy.

"It's been three weeks Victoria and you haven't returned any of my calls or came to work. I know you are going through a tough time right now, but we need you at work. The paper work isn't going to take care of its self."

My Boss said.

"Henry, sir I am going to be honest, I don't care, and right now I just want to be alone."

I said before slamming the door in his face.

A few minutes later I received a text saying that I was fired and to come clean out my office immediately. I didn't even let it phase me; instead I threw my phone on the couch and opened another carton of ice cream. A few hours later I got the urge that someone was watching me. I shrugged it off and realized that I smelled something that stunk.

After realizing that the stink was myself, I decided that maybe it was time to get a shower.

I got up from the couch and headed upstairs to the bathroom. I stripped down and turned on my shower to the hottest setting, I stepped in took a breath, feeling relaxed as the steaming water ran down my back. As I stood there with my eyes closed I thought about nanny and how much I missed her. I finished my shower and got dressed because I had decided that maybe a drive would help me feel a little better.

I got into my car; I didn't know where I was going to go I just knew that I wanted to drive. Before long I realized that I had driven to the graveyard. I slowly got out of my car and walked over to her headstone that had a newly engraved hummingbird on it because she absolutely loved hummingbirds. I took a breath and fell to my knees crying thinking about all the talks we shared over coloring posters and drinking coffee.

I sat there on the ground sobbing until my eyes were all out of tears.

I had lost my most favorite person in the world, I had no one to talk to and I had lost my job. My life was out of control and falling apart and I had no idea how to stop it. As I started to get up I whispered,

"I love you up to the moon."

Normally she would say "and back again" but this time I didn't hear it. It was something we had said to each other since I was a kid; it was part of our special bond.

When I got back home, I was numb, I didn't want to be alive anymore, I just wanted my life to end because without her here I felt like my life wasn't worth living. I went in my house, locked the door behind me and then sat down and wrote a powerful goodbye letter. I sealed it in an envelope and stuck it on the table where I knew it would be found.

I grabbed a kitchen knife and went to the bedroom, slamming the door shut. I grabbed my Bible and sat down on the bed with the knife in one hand and the bible in the other. I took a breath while holding the knife to my throat. I whispered the words,

"I'm sorry nanny forgive me."

As I started to push the knife to my throat a light coming from my closet caught my attention. I lowered the knife and hopped off the bed slowly moving to my closet. I pulled the door open to find nothing; it was organized like always except for the light. I took a step forward and heard the door shut behind me. As I turned back around I saw another door, I touched the handle and turned slowly.

Chapter 2

I gasped as it opened, I walked out and I was in HEAVEN! Actual heaven just liked the bible described. I looked around in amazement and saw the clouds, blue skies and straight ahead of me was the pearly gates and the streets made of gold. Standing at the gates was an angel dressed in white with a gold halo.

"Am I dead?"

I asked myself?

I approached the gates not knowing what was going to happen next.

I smiled at the angel and she smiled and with a kind voice said,

"This way Victoria"

I walked with her down the road made of pure gold. It was so beautiful. I knew now why this place was called heaven. We stopped in front of a little emerald cottage by a river and I was told what I desired was inside. Confusingly, I walked up the steps and before I could knock the door flew open. Before I walked in I heard,

"Tori Lynn"

There was only one person that called me that. I walked in and there she was, my nanny, she was sitting on a couch made of pure emerald and drinking a cup of coffee. At that moment I couldn't breath I stood there with a tear rolling down my cheek.

"Well, now, are you just going to stand there or are you going to come give me a hug?"

Nanny asked.

I quickly ran over to her and before I knew it our arms was wrapped around each other.

"You are here, you're really here."

I said.

"Yes, honey, I am here and I love you. I'm not so happy you were going to try and kill yourself though."

She said.

I looked up at her confused.

"Your not dead Tori, you are still very much alive. Think of this as a gift. You are receiving something that other's have dreamed of, a chance to visit heaven."

I stood there speechless. I didn't know what to say. All I could do was cry. I sat down with my nanny and after a few minutes I finally spoke.

"Nanny, it's beautiful here, I see why it's called heaven."

"Yes, it's a wonderful place and now I have another gift, because you are all alone right now and having a hard time you can come visit me anytime until you don't need me anymore."

"Really? Oh, thank you nanny, I will be here everyday."

I said ecstatically.

"Now hold on a minute there are some rules. One you can't tell anyone. This is our little secret and again, it's only until you don't need me to guide you anymore."

Nanny said.

"Yes, Mam, I understand, but how will I get here?"

I asked.

"The same way you got here earlier the back of your closet. Now tell me about your job and everything."

I began explaining how I distanced myself from everyone, how depressed I was and how I had lost my job. We talked for what seemed like hours about what I should do and other things. Then nanny asked,

"Tori would you like to meet some people?"

"Sure"

I answered.

Nanny then led me out of the cottage to the streets. As we walked down the golden road I noticed that there were a lot of cottages. We continued walking until we reached a big castle made of gold.

"Is this? Are we?"

I asked.

Nanny smiled as she opened the door and pushed it open. I took a breath and walked in beside her nervously.

I looked around and saw a room made of pure crystal, a throne made of gold, angels playing music and tables of food everywhere. It was the most beautiful thing I had ever seen and I didn't want to ever leave. I sat down waiting on nanny and listened to a male angel playing Amazing Grace on a harp.

I started humming with the music, and started singing softly. When the angel quit playing he looked at me and smiled.

"You have a beautiful voice, Tori, my name is Gabriel."

I smiled and admired his beauty. Then I heard nanny call over to me.

"Tori come with me."

She said as she grabbed my hand.

We walked over to where the throne of gold was. As I admired its beauty I noticed a man dressed in white clothing sitting there. I instantly knew who it was and I began to softly weep. Nanny looked at me smiling and said,

"It's ok Tori, I wept too."

As we reached him I felt myself dropping to my knees and bowing my head. Feeling his presence I had never felt more alive. My heart felt whole again instead of like something was missing.

"Lift your head, Tori."

He said softly.

As I lifted my head and stood I looked into his eyes and felt calm.

He was the most beautiful thing that I had ever seen. His entire body had a light glow to it and a safety like feeling radiated from him.

"Welcome my child, are you liking it here?"

He asked.

I simply nodded because I couldn't speak.

"You are very lucky Tori, no one living has ever been able to visit.

You have the gift that many people would love to have. You were granted this gift because your nanny and I felt like you needed it. You will be able to continue coming until you don't need to anymore. But in return you have to fight to continue to live your life Tori. Many great things are coming your way. You just have to look for signs and follow your heart."

He said with a calm, sincere voice.

He then handed me a cross necklace and told me to get back to just hold the cross against my chest, which was easier than going into my closet and it would bring me as long as I needed it but once I didn't need it anymore it would just be an ordinary necklace. I nodded in understanding and said thank you. He then hugged me and told me he believed in me.

After meeting the one and only holy one I enjoyed a little bit longer with nanny. When it was time to go I hugged her tight, held the cross and closed my eyes. When I opened them again, I was back in my bedroom. I let out a sigh of relief and felt much better because I now knew I wasn't alone.

Chapter 3

I awoke the next morning feeling whole again and happier than I had been. At first I thought that I had been dreaming, but then I looked down and felt the necklace and I knew instantly that it had all been real. Knowing that I could go back and visit my nanny made me feel at peace and it didn't hurt as much. I knew it was time to start putting my life back together.

I got up, got in the shower, got dressed and headed downstairs to the kitchen. Feeling refreshed, I fixed me a jumbo pot of coffee and some fried eggs and sausage. While eating I searched online for job openings in my area since I was now unemployed. I searched for what seemed like hours on Indeed.com and nothing listed was anything I could do.

I sighed and closed my computer. "Maybe walking around town will help." I thought to myself.

I put my dishes in the sink and grabbed my car keys and left. I knew that at my previous job I was in charge of having the bills ready and printed for the insurance company. I didn't really enjoy it, but at least it was a job. Maybe now I could find something that I actually enjoy doing. I took a breath and asked nanny to point me in the right direction.

I started driving through downtown Raleigh and after seeing all the traffic decided that it might be best to park and walk. I threw my keys in my purse, locked the doors and got out. I inhaled the cool fall breeze and walked across the street to the sidewalk. I was right walking made me feel even better.

I noticed that a lot of the shops had fall decorations up and was getting ready for the annual fall festival next week. October was my favorite time of the year and I couldn't believe I had been missing it. I kept walking not really thinking about where I was going when a giant poster in a window caught my eye.

It was a COMING SOON sign and beneath it was the words LOOKING FOR HELP. It was a new place that was fixing to open up. I didn't know why, but at that moment I seemed very interested. I grabbed the door handle and pushed it open. As it opened a gust of wind came back and about knocked me over. I softly shut the door behind me and as I began to turn around I heard,

"Welcome to Keply's Books, I'll be right with you."

I quickly noticed all the books and the Halloween themed decorations around the store. The store was warm and smelled like pumpkin I instantly felt at home. I was walking to the fiction section when someone started speaking.

"Hello, I'm Eric, Keply's grandson, how may I help you?"

I smiled at the young man; he seemed to be my age and was very handsome. He was a couple inches taller than me with dark hair, brown eyes and very tan skin. He looked like he had been sunbathing on a beach.

"Hello, my name is Tori, I noticed your help wanted sign out front."

I said, smiling.

"Oh well let me get my Grandpa for you, he is in the back unpacking books."

I heard him say while walking away.

I continued to look at the shop in amazement and after a few minutes an older gentleman with a warm smile appeared. He looked to be in his sixties, had dark hair that was turning gray and was using a cane. I quickly grabbed the box from him that he was trying to carry with one hand.

"Hello, my grandson said you're here about a job correct?" The man asked.

I nodded and replied with,

"Yes, sir"

"Alright, if you can put these books on the shelf in the right spot and order, then you can have the job."

Mr. Keply said.

I smiled and opened the box. It was a box of periodicals, I sighed in relief because periodical organization is something I actually had no problem with. I grabbed a few from the stack and walked over to the periodical section and in minutes I had the entire section in the right order and neatly organized.

"I'm impressed, you have the job, and may I ask your name?"

"Victoria but everyone calls me Tori."

I said.

"Well, Tori you have yourself a job. What days and hours can you work?"

"I'm available any time you need me."

"Good you can start right now, I need a break, and my back isn't as strong as it used to be."

Mr. Keply said while sitting down.

I smiled and went in the back to grab a few more boxes to start unpacking. As I walked into the back of the store I noticed Eric bringing in boxes from outside and setting them down.

"Would you like some help with that?"

I asked.

"No, I'm fine, but thanks though. So I take it my Grandpa just hired you."

"Yes, my name is Tori."

I said while shaking his hand. I looked into his eyes while shaking his hand and felt an instant attraction. Feeling that he could sense it, I quickly pulled away blushing.

"Well, Tori welcome to Keply's books."

Eric said before turning away to unload more books. I watched him for a moment and noticed that he had very nice muscles. I told myself no and quickly got to work unpacking and organizing books.

Chapter 4

When I arrived home it was after six and I was tired. I had ended up unloading and organizing 25 boxes of books and filling out paperwork.

Mr. Keply was impressed, we agreed that I would work Tuesday through Saturday from 10 to 6. The pay wasn't bad either.

I really enjoyed working with books and Eric and Mr. Keply were friendly as well. I had a feeling that I had found my permanent job.

I was exhausted but hungry, so I ordered a pizza and decided to call my mom.

She seemed happy to hear from me and asked me how I was doing.

We talked for a good little while about my new job and what my plans were for Thanksgiving. By the time we hung up we had planned on her coming over and us spending Thanksgiving together.

After eating and having a glass of wine I went upstairs and crawled into bed with a book. I figured that I would read a good book before bed to try and relax me, but boy I was wrong because every time I would turn a page Eric would pop into my mind. I couldn't help it; he was so fine, his dark hair, eyes and his muscles. Seeing the muscles in his arms today made me wonder if he was muscular all over. I noticed he wasn't wearing a ring, but knowing my luck, he was probably taken. I pushed it from my head; I didn't need a man right now anyway.

I realized I wasn't going to get to sleep anytime soon so I decided that I would make a visit. I grabbed my necklace with one hand and took a deep breath and shut my eyes. When I opened my eyes again, I was back in heaven at the gates. The beauty of the gates caught my attention again.

I smiled at the angel that had greeted me before and walked down the golden road to the cottage by the lake where the angel had taken me before.

Before I could knock the door flew open again and nanny was waiting in the doorway with two cups of coffee in her hand.

"It's about time you got here."

She said smiling.

I smiled back at her took a cup out of her hand and followed her to a deck attached to the back of the cottage. It was absolutely breath taking because as soon as you walked out it was facing the lake and it was a scene like no other. The water was so clear that you could literally see a lot of fish, plants and frogs as soon as you glanced down.

"Nanny it is absolutely gorgeous out here and peaceful too."

I said while sitting down at the outside table.

"Yes, I love it and peaceful it is. After all, my life I now understand why heaven is called heaven. You may not get to stay here with me now, but one day you will and we will be able to come out here all the time together."

She said while grabbing my hand and smiling at me.

I took a sip of my coffee and looked out across the lake thinking about how nanny was so lucky to be here. She has no worries, was at peace and was never alone. At that moment I felt guilty for how I had felt before.

"Tori what's wrong? And don't say nothing because I can see it in your face."

I smiled at her and told her how I was now feeling guilty about missing her so much and about almost taking my life because I didn't get to say goodbye. When I should have been overjoyed that she was in a place where she would never be sad, worried or sick again.

"Tori Lynn, don't you dare feel guilty, everyone deals with grief differently. I didn't wait for you to arrive at your mom's because I knew it would be harder on you watching me take my last breath than you knowing that my last words to you were I love you and to take care of yourself, so don't you dare feel guilty."

Nanny said while taking my face in her hand and kissing my forehead. I knew she was right, so while holding back tears I just nodded.

"Now tell me about this new job and that grandson of Mr. Keply's."

I began to tell her about how I just went for a drive and ended up there and when I walked it how at home I felt. She smiled as I lit up telling her. I also told her about how mom and I made plans for Thanksgiving.

"That's awesome, I am proud of you Tori. See I told you that you could do anything you set your mind to. Now tell me about this Eric, he's handsome."

"Well, there isn't much to tell, I only just met him. But he is very good looking and sweet from what I can tell and those muscles are very dreamy."

I said while blushing.

"I say go for it. You need someone to keep you company, even if it is just friendship. Besides, I want great grandchildren, one day."

Nanny said while taking a sip of coffee and looking at me.

I just looked at her and smiled. Even in heaven, she was still her comical, joyful self, which I loved. We talked for a little bit longer when she said something that I dreaded hearing but I knew was coming.

"You're almost to where you don't need me Tori which was the goal.

You get one more visit after this one, and then you won't be able to come back until it's your time. After the next time your necklace will turn into a normal necklace, but don't forget I will always be with you. Now run along, you have work soon."

Nanny said while giving me a great bear hug. I kissed her cheek and told her,

"I love you up to the moon…"

Then she looked at me and said,

"And back again."

After we said goodbye, I went back home and went into a deep sleep. I woke up the next morning feeling relaxed and ready for the day.

I quickly got dressed, drank a few cups of coffee and left.

When I arrived at the shop Eric was already there and he looked even more handsome today than he did yesterday. He was wearing a red NC State football shirt today with jeans. I smiled at him and helped him unload some books. When he saw me, his eyes lit up and he flashed me a smile.

As I helped him unload the last of the boxes I noticed Mr. Keply standing in the corner watching us.

"Well, now, you two seem to make a great team.

Mr. Keply said, smiling.

After a few hours of unloading boxes and trying to get them catalogued I headed home for the day. I didn't get to talk to Eric much today because he had left a little bit before I did. He was so handsome but I highly doubted that he would be interested in me.

When I got home, I turned on some music and went upstairs to use the bathroom. I was daydreaming and hadn't noticed until heading back downstairs that someone was knocking on the door.

I opened the door to find Eric standing there in his red NC State T-Shirt, Blue Jeans and cowboy boots. He looked so handsome and he smelled great too. I could tell instantly that he was either wearing old spice deodorant or he was using old spice body wash.

"Hey, I've been knocking for a few minutes."

He said softly.

"Sorry I was upstairs in the bathroom."

I said.

"Oh, sorry, I was starting to think you didn't want to see me."

He said while looking down at his shoe.

"No, don't think that, Come on in and have a seat.

I said while walking over to my couch and turning down the music.

So what's up?"

I asked.

"Oh, nothing, I um came because my Grandpa told me I should."

He said shyly. I looked at him confusingly, but immediately started wondering why.

"Is there something wrong?"

I asked.

"No, there's nothing wrong that I know of. I came over to ask if you would like to go out on a date with me tonight because I think you're gorgeous."

He said while trying not to look at me.

I smiled and while looking into his eyes said,

"Sure, just give me a few minutes to get dressed."

His eyes and face lit up. He may look big and bad, but I could see he was a gentle kitten with a shy side. Maybe nanny was on to something.

I told him to give a few minutes while I changed. I quickly rushed upstairs and slipped on a cute top with some jeans, brushed my curly brown hair and threw on some makeup to bring out my green eyes more.

When I walked back downstairs, he was looking at the pictures that I had on my wall. I smiled and asked him,

"Are you ready?"

Once he turned around and saw me he started blushing and I could tell he was impressed. I quickly learned that he was quite the gentleman because he held the door open for me while I walked out of my house and while I got in his truck.

He was driving one of my favorite types of trucks, a black dodge ram. I looked around the inside at the leather interior and his CD

collection, which was mainly old country and rock. I really liked what I was seeing. On the way to where ever we were going we talked and sung along to Alabama and Def Leppard.

He was really easy to talk to, which I liked and as we talked we found out we had quite a lot of things in common, So much that I started to wonder if nanny had something to do with this as well. I asked him where we were headed and with a smile he said,

"It's a surprise."

I trusted him, which felt odd because I hadn't trusted any man since my bad break up with my ex. He saw that I was thinking hard about something and asked if everything was ok.

"Yes, everything is fine, I just haven't dated anyone since my bad break up last year."

I said softly.

"Well, if it makes you feel better, I haven't dated anyone in a while either. I had a bad break up last year as well. My fiancé who I had been with since high school cheated on me with my now ex best friend."

"Damn, I'm sorry to hear that, if you want we can consider this not as a date just a friendly outing."

I said, hoping he would disagree.

"Nope, that's ancient history and why wouldn't I want this to be a date? I think you're amazing so far."

Eric said while grabbing my hand.

I just smiled, his hand in mine felt right, so I just left it there. A few moments later as we were pulling off the road onto a dirt driveway, I heard, "We're here."

I was a little confused at first because all I saw was woods until I noticed the woods opened up into a big field with a river running through it. Straight ahead was a big red barn covered in orange lights.

It looked perfect.

"It's beautiful"

"There's more do you want to see?"

Eric asked while getting out of the truck.

I nodded and followed him. He grabbed me by the hand and led me to the barn. As we approached I heard music playing as we approached closer I looked inside and saw that a stack of hay bails had been made into chairs and a blanket sitting on the ground in-between them with a picnic basket and wine glasses sitting on it.

I was amazed because this was beyond perfect. This was way more romantic than any restaurant could ever be. It's like he just knew I would say yes to his offer.

"I brought you here because I felt like this would be a better first date, then the steak house I originally thought about. I didn't want you to think I was just like everyone else."

"Eric, it's perfect."

I said while touching his face.

I looked into his eyes and felt again that I had scored big. We then sat down on his hay chairs; he opened the picnic basket and pulled out a bottle of Black River Wine made from Duplin Winery.

He poured us both a glass and then pulled out some plates, napkins and silverware. Smiling, he then started to pull out some food. Next he pulled out some containers of steak, Mac n cheese and baked potatoes.

It all smelled delicious. After distributing them onto our plates, he said,

"I like to cook."

"All of this looks and smells amazing. You sure do know how to get into a woman's heart, that's for sure."

I said while raising my wine glass.

He blushed as I took my first bite of steak, which was delicious. It was one of the best steaks that I had ever tasted. After we got through eating, he surprised me again by pulling out a guitar. He started playing and singing George Straits "Check Yes or No."

What the heck is going on? I asked myself because this felt too good to be true. Sitting in front of me was a man that was sweet, handsome, romantic, and he could cook and sing. As I was thinking all this I heard nanny in my head,

"Nothing is too good for you."

When Eric quit playing I clapped my hands and told him that he was great.

"I'm not that good, it's just a hobby."

"Are you kidding, that was amazing. Not everyone can pull off George like that."

"Would you like to dance?"

He asked, smiling.

"Sure, I would love to."

I grabbed his hand and he pulled me into him. He smelled so good so I just let myself fall deeper into him. We danced for a while to every song that seemed to come on the radio. This felt like a fairy tale and I knew I never wanted it to end.

I woke up the next morning to my alarm clock. I turned it off and wondered if that date had been a dream. I sat up, stretching and walked across the hall to the bathroom and over to my shower, I dropped my nightgown and stepped in still half asleep. I stood under the hot water with my eyes closed, letting the water wake me up while thinking about Eric and how perfect he was.

I was lost in thought when I heard someone walking into the bathroom. It startled me so I peeped around the curtain to find Eric releasing his waters of mankind. He was still half asleep as well, so it kind of startled both of us.

"Oh my gosh, I am so sorry, I didn't realize you were in here."

He said apologetically.

"I'm going to be honest, I forgot you were still here."

I said while covering myself with the shower curtain.

"Not used to people being over?"

"No not really I said. Hang on and I will be out in just a minute."

I said while turning off the water and reaching for a towel that I ended up dropping.

"Here, let me get that for you."

Eric said while reaching down to get it.

After handing me the towel I quickly wrapped myself in it and stepped out of the shower. His hair was a mess and he looked so sexy shirtless. I was trying to remember what else had happened last night.

"Um, Eric doesn't get mad at me for asking, but my mind is blank."

He chuckled a little.

"It's alright, we came back here after we left the barn last night and finished the two other bottles of wine that I had. You told me to stay so I slept on your couch, which isn't that comfy by the way."

"Yeah, I've been meaning to get a new one. Um, we didn't, you know, did we?"

I asked, looking down.

"No, I was raised to be a gentleman, so sex on the first date is not a thing for me."

He said while looking at me.

"Oh, well that is one thing I like about you."

I said while still holding the towel around me.

Eric smiled at me and walked out of the bathroom. I took a breath and walked out across the hall to my room. I shut the door, dropped the towel and quickly got dressed. I threw on a pair of jeans and a light blue T-shirt, slid on my flip-flops and headed downstairs.

Eric was sitting on the couch watching CMT on TV with his shirt back on. I pushed the thought of taking it back off of him out of my mind and walked to the kitchen to put some coffee on.

"Would you like a cup of coffee?"

I asked him.

"Oh yes, I would love some. I might wake up then."

He said while walking into the kitchen.

Opening up the fridge, I pulled out my pumpkin spice creamer and the white chocolate raspberry creamer. I then grabbed two cups out of the cabinet and handed one to him. I poured coffee into my cup, added some pumpkin spice creamer and two tablespoons of sugar. I then sat down at the table and watched as he did the same.

"So you like pumpkin spice as well."

I said.

"I love pumpkin everything. That's one of the reasons I love this time of year. Pumpkins, color, cool weather and football."

Eric said while taking a sip of coffee.

"Really? I love football. Who's your favorite team?"

I asked.

"Besides NC State, I would have to say The Panthers and The Bronco's."

I was shocked because those were my two favorite teams as well. I started to realize that maybe I had found the one that I was meant to be with because we seemed to have everything in common.

"The reason you keep seeing all this NC State stuff is because I went there and graduated last year. I played football for them up until I blew out my knee my junior year. I was impressing scouts too, but obviously it wasn't meant to be."

He said, looking sad.

After we finished our coffee, he left to go home and change and I headed on to work. I made it to the shop before Eric did and Mr.

Keply had been already in the shop organizing books. He looked tired but motivated. I walked in, set my purse behind the counter and got his attention.

"Good morning Tori, I didn't see you come in, I was too focused on these two books."

He said while holding them in his hands.

"What's so confusing?"

I asked while looking at the old books.

"They are both by the same author, but I can't seem to figure out which one goes first because the titles are both faded and my eyesight isn't as good as it used to be."

I took the books from him and told him not to worry about it.

He was right though, those books were so old that it took me a couple minutes to figure out what they said.

Eric came in a few minutes later with more coffee and pumpkin doughnuts. I smiled and thought to myself,

"This man is trying very hard."

I walked over and grabbed a cup of coffee and a doughnut and walked into the back office with Mr. Keply who was trying to catalogue the books that was in the box that he was unpacking. He smiled when he saw Eric and the doughnuts.

"I hate coffee, but I sure do love doughnuts."

Mr. Keply said, smiling.

We enjoyed the doughnuts and got to work. I took over the cataloging, which meant I wrote down the title of every book under the name of its author in the order like it would be put on the shelf after putting them in order in the box. It was an easy way of organization and classification.

Once I was done, Eric took the books and placed them in the correct order on the shelves while Mr. Keply was straightening up the front of the shop. I knew I hadn't been here that long but all three of us made a good team.

A couple hours later when we decided to take a lunch break Mr. Keply asked,

"So Tori, how did your date go with my grandson? I just knew you would say yes. Did he treat you right?"

I looked at Eric and smiled.

"Yes, Mr. Keply, he was a real gentleman last night. He took me on a very romantic date."

"That's good, I tried raising him right. After his momma died, his grandmother and I was all he had."

"Well, I think you raised a fine young man, and I think I would like to go out with him again if that's alright with you."

I watched Mr. Keply's face light up as I said that and it made me feel good.

"I would love that, he needs a good woman in his life like you because I won't be around much longer and I don't want him to be alone."

He said while grabbing my hand.

Chapter 6

Since that day a week ago Eric and I have been by each other's side. We spent our days off helping his Grandpa around his farm, which I loved, and finding me a more comfortable couch. I ended up going with a leather couch from Big Lots.

It was finally the day of the festival and the grand opening day for the bookstore. Mr. Keply, Eric and I were all excited. The store had multiple genres to choose from, from kids fiction and adult fiction all the way to non-fiction and biographies. Everything was neatly organized and everything looked great.

To grab people's attention Eric spent last night hanging up orange lights around the store sign. I decorated the front of the store with a fall theme, I sat cute little pumpkin and bat figurines in the windows set out some artificial candles on the tables after covering them with black table clothes and Eric even brought my old couch over for people to sit on. Mr. Keply even put an orange and black rug down on the carpet.

As the festival started people started walking down the sidewalks and a few would stop and stare in amazement at all the decorations. About an hour after all the festivities began we got our very first costumer. It was an older woman, she was very nice and she seemed to have an eye out for Mr. Keply. She introduced herself as Miss Carol Barnett and spent a good little bit walking around admiring the shop. After looking at all the books she got excited because she found A Tale of Two Kitties by her favorite author Sofie Kelly that she had been wanting to read for a while now. She took it off the shelf and walked over to the cash register.

"I have been waiting so long to read this book. You guys have a great selection I will definitely be back.

She said sounding excited.

After she left more people started coming in to look around and ask questions. A few people even started reading inside the shop. We ended up making over two hundred dollars in profit before we closed at three.

We closed early so we could all enjoy the festival.

After locking up the store Eric grabbed my hand and we started walking the festival. We stopped at the main stage to listen to some local music. We then grabbed some barbeque that was a little pricey, but worth every penny. After eating, we walked around for a bit looking at all the vendors. I spotted a vendor selling jewelry and went to look.

I noticed a ring that looked absolutely stunning. It had a big garnet stone in the middle with a diamond on each side. It was breath taking but it costed a fortune because it was real gold. I didn't even bother trying it on because I knew I couldn't afford it. I sighed softly and kept walking. We were walking when people started running past us to the other stage. Eric and I looked at each other and went to try and see what everyone was in a rush about.

When we reached the stage I noticed right away why everyone was crowding around. Garner's own Scotty Mccreery was setting up to take the stage. He introduced himself and started to sing. I froze when he started because he started singing "Hello Darlin" by Conway Twitty.

That song was one of my favorites and it had been nanny's song and mine. We would sing it to one another when I was growing up. Scotty wasn't Conway by any means, but he had been the only other person I knew of that could pull the song off and it not sound horrible.

I started to softly sing along while trying not to cry. Eric noticed and asked me what was wrong and I explained to him. He understood and pulled me into him. After Scotty finished his first song he went on to his next and Eric and I started to dance. We kept watching and listening for a few more minutes, and then we started walking again.

Around six we decided to call it a day and we headed back to my house. We ordered some pizza from Pizza Hut, had some wine and cuddled up on the couch to watch some Netflix. I felt comfortable lying in his arms because he was warm like a blanket. I yawned quietly and buried my head into his chest and fell asleep.

While asleep, I started dreaming about him proposing to me in a room with his Grandpa, my mom and the ring that I saw today. It was perfect. I felt happiness and love in this dream. The only thing missing was nanny. I woke up later that night still in his arms. He was asleep, so I turned off the TV and the lights and closed my eyes again thinking that maybe one day that dream would come true.

When I woke up again, it was morning and Eric was snoring loudly with his mouth hanging open. I smiled and closed his mouth; he woke up instantly and started looking around while stretching.

"Good morning."

I said while looking at him.

"Good morning beautiful. I guess we were more tired than we thought last night."

He said while sitting up.

"I guess so, but I'm not complaining, I was comfy."

I said while heading to the kitchen to start some coffee. I looked at the calendar and noticed that tomorrow night was Halloween and I still hadn't got a costume or any candy for trick or treaters. I quickly wrote down on a sheet of paper that I needed to do that today and started to make two cups of coffee. I grabbed the cups and headed back into the living room

I handed him a cup and sat down beside him. I sipped on my coffee while it cooled off.

I have to go by Wal-Mart later for my Halloween costume and some candy would you like to go with me?"

I asked.

"Sure, what are you thinking about dressing up as?"

Eric asked.

"I'm not sure, I thought about possibly a vampire."

"Interesting, I could be Dracula and you could be my lady."

Eric said while smiling.

"Maybe, I'll think about it."

I said while putting the cups in the sink and heading upstairs.

Once reached the bathroom, I washed myself off and slipped on a comfy sweater dress. I brushed my hair, put on some deodorant and headed back downstairs. As I was coming down the stairs, I heard Eric talking to someone.

"Yeah man, if it's alright with my girl we will be there tomorrow night. I can't wait for you to meet her, she is amazing."

I smiled, but wondered whom he was talking to. When he got off the phone I asked,

"Who was that? I don't mean to pry I'm just curious."

"It was one of my buddies from state, he is throwing a party tomorrow night and wanted to know if I wanted to come. I told him that is was up to you."

"Sure we can, that is if you want me to. I can just leave the candy out on the porch for the kiddos."

I said.

"Great, I think you will really like Nate. He's like me in a lot of ways. We played on the team together. Nate was the quarterback and I was a linebacker."

"I'm sure I will."

I said while wrapping my arms around him and finally kissing him softly. That was out first kiss and it felt perfect.

"Wow, I was waiting for that, but I didn't know it was going to be that great."

Eric said while kissing me again.

We took his truck to Wal-Mart, we went in and grabbed a big bag of candy and spent the next thirty minutes looking for the perfect costume. He found his Dracula costume that came with face paint. I found my costume as well; it came with a black dress, a black wig and fangs. We were both happy with what we found and on the way out I grabbed two plastic pumpkins to put the candy in.

We left and spent the rest of the day at my house cleaning and straightening everything up. That evening I decided to cook him dinner, I made baked Italian pork chops, Mac and cheese and broccoli.

It all tasted absolutely delicious.

"Where did you get these cooking skills?"

"I learned from my nanny, she always loved to cook and she never cooked light either."

I said while remembering all the delicious meals that my nanny had made. Especially at Thanksgiving and Christmas.

"Oh, I figure you would have said your mom."

"Nope, mom never really did and still doesn't like cooking very much. Don't get me wrong, she would occasionally cook a big meal, but for the most part she, just like getting things that she could quickly throw together. Her country style steak and mashed taters are to die for though. I'll try and get her to make some for Thanksgiving."

I said while lost in thought.

Eric and I spent the next day getting candy and things ready for trick or treaters. We distributed the candy we bought into two buckets and made a sign that said two pieces per child. Before we headed to the party, we went and checked on Mr. Keply.

When we got to the farm Mr. Keply was outside feeding his chickens and horses. He had some beautiful horses. My favorite was the solid white mare with the black mane. Her name was Beauty and believe me she knew it too.

"Well, don't you two look nice?"

Mr. Keply said after giving Beauty an apple.

"Thanks Grandpa, were headed to a party, I just wanted to come check on you before we went."

"I'm fine Eric, you two go have some fun, just remember to be safe and if for some reason both of you should have too much to drink call me."

I smiled and nodded.

Mr. Keply was great, but I was scared. I started feeling like everything was happening so fast. Mr. Keply felt like a dad to me and Eric was so amazing. When he wasn't with me he was constantly on my mind. When I say his name or think about him my heart would feel tight in my Chest and I would automatically feel happy. "Is this love?" I wondered

When we got back in the truck Eric could tell something was bothering me. But I didn't know how to tell him except for just telling him like it is.

"Tori, are you ok?"

"Yes, I'm fine, I think, I want to tell you something, but I'm kind of afraid to because it seems too soon and like everything is happening so fast."

I said, mumbling.

Eric smiled, took my hand and looked me straight in the eye.

"I love you Tori."

I smiled. He said it and I didn't even have to.

"I love you Eric."

I said while he kissed my hand.

Chapter 7

We arrived at the party around eight and it was already packed.

Nate lived in one of the biggest houses just out of the city limits. I automatically felt out of place because being rich was definitely not a category that I fell under.

Eric grabbed my hand and as we walked in I instantly felt like I was at a college frat party. The music was extremely loud but at least it was decent music. Eric and I walked into the next room when we heard,

"Eric my man it has been a while."

Eric looked over his shoulder and noticed that someone was coming down the stairs.

"Hey Nate, Eric said while slapping his hand. How have you been buddy?"

"I've been great, how are you? Still helping out your grandpa? And who is this with you?"

Nate asked.

"Nate, this is my girlfriend Tori and of course I'm still helping my grandpa he's all the family I have left. My grandpa actually just opened a bookshop up town. You should come check it out sometime. Tori and I both work there so one of us will always be there."

Nate started to rattle on about something when he got distracted because someone broke an expensive flower vase. Eric got us both some punch and introduced me to the rest of the guys that he played football with. I really enjoyed meeting them; they all seemed down to earth.

Eric and I were both having a good time until some guy came up and grabbed my butt from behind.

"Hey man, watch it."

I said while turning around.

Eric quickly whirled around and his face instantly changed.

"Still causing trouble Brandon?"

Eric asked.

"I'm surprised you're here after everything that happened between you and Kathleen and all. But I see you moved on you have yourself another beautiful woman Eric."

Brandon said while eyeballing me.

"Back off Brandon, What happened is over and done with, let it go."

Eric said in a deeper voice.

"Oh, I let it go, but have you and Kathleen let it go?"

Brandon said, smirking.

At that moment I got in between them two because I could tell Eric was getting mad and getting ready to hit him. I pulled Eric away so he could cool off some.

"I'm going to go upstairs and use the bathroom. Are you ok?"

I smiled at him and assured him that I was fine. As he walked upstairs, I made me another cup of punch and sat down on Nate's couch. As I sat waiting for Eric I started scrolling through Facebook on my phone. Soon five minutes went by and Eric still hadn't come back so I decided to go upstairs to check on him.

When I reached the top of the stairs, I still saw no signs of Eric and no one was in the bathroom. I suddenly started to panic and wonder if he had ditched me. As I turned to leave I noticed someone in the corner behind the piano and when I noticed whom it was my heart shattered.

Eric was in the corner by the window with another woman. She was gorgeous and had wavy blonde hair and their lips were locked. I went over pushed her off of him and slapped him in the face.

"How could you, just hours after I told you that I loved you."

I quickly raced down the stairs and out of the house while slamming the door behind me. I ran down the street sobbing not caring about where I was going. I knew that I just had to get away from there. I finally admitted that I loved that man and he goes and does this.

My entire make up was coming off my face, but I didn't care. I found a large oak tree and sat down against it trying to calm myself down. I cried until I couldn't cry anymore. I took a deep breath and called an Uber to come and get me.

I arrived back home around 11 that night since it took longer for me to get home than it was to get there. I kind of spilled all of my hurt and anger to the Uber driver. She was empathetic and said that she probably would have done more than slap him.

When I got in my house I ripped the costume off and threw everything on my couch and then I ran upstairs into the bathroom.

I washed off the rest of the make up that hadn't already came off and went and jumped into bed. I was wearing nothing but my bra and underwear, but I didn't care. I let all of my emotions out onto my pillow and eventually fell asleep.

I woke up to my nanny's voice in my ear.

"Open your eyes, Tori."

I quickly opened my eyes and saw that I was in my nightgown in nanny's cottage on her emerald couch. I sat up and she wiped a tear from my eye. Don't cry Tori, I know your upset, but there is much you don't know.

I looked at her confused.

"Come with me and I will show you."

Nanny then grabbed my hand and took me through her cottage to a big mirror in her room. She made me sit in front of the mirror.

"Now watch."

She said.

As I begin to look at the mirror it started to change colors and I saw Eric, we were at the party. I saw him go upstairs into the bathroom and come out. I knew where this was going and I didn't want to watch it all over again but nanny pointed and I looked.

After he came out the blonde came up behind him and spun him around.

"Hey stranger, Brandon told me that you were here."

"What do you want Kathleen?"

Eric asked.

"I thought we should talk."

Kathleen said while pushing him into the corner.

"There is nothing to talk about Kathleen we are over and done. I have moved on with a woman that is ten times the woman you are."

As Eric began to move, Kathleen pulled him into her and kissed him as I was walking up the stairs. I watched as I shoved her and slapped him. I instantly felt bad because I didn't let him explain. I then watched Eric run down the stairs and reach the door after I had run and hid next to the tree. I saw him call for me and punch his truck in frustration.

He then got in his truck and tried calling me. I watched as he started blaming himself, saying that he should have never agreed to go to that party. That I was his world now and that how he felt like he had just lost me. Before the mirror went blank I saw him pull up to his Grandpas.

"Oh, Nanny, I feel so ashamed."

I said.

"Don't be, you didn't know the truth, I think you should of let him explain before you slapped him though."

Nanny said, smiling.

"Nanny I never thought I would say this, but I love Eric so much, he's so wonderful."

"I know Tori and believe me he loves you too. I knew he was perfect for you that's why I led you to that bookstore. You deserve someone that is going to treat you like a queen and Tori my dear that is Eric."

"So I was right, I knew you had something to do with me finding the book store and Eric. He is amazing; he hasn't pressured me into doing anything that I don't want to do. We've been taking things slow because I don't want to lose him."

"Well, now I guess you know what you need to do soon because he's desperately trying to get a hold of you. But right now he's going to stop and leave you alone until morning. But now in the morning you need to go talk to him"

I smiled, and gave nanny a big hug.

"Okay, but before I go since I won't be able to come back how about one last game of UNO?"

Nanny smiled a big grin and said

"Game on."

Nanny invited a few people to play with us, including Eric's mother and my great grandmother. Eric's mother looked just like him and she was really sweet. I found out her name was Amelia and she had passed away because of cancer. My great grandmother and I also had a good conversation. She asked me,

"Still eating snow cream every winter?"

I smiled at her and said,

"Yes Mam."

"Yeah, I used to feed that stuff to your little butt when you were a baby. You loved it, but your daddy had a fit."

I laughed and after my great grandmother winning the game and promising Amelia that I would take care of her son I kissed them all goodbye and gave them a big hug. Then I looked at nanny gave her a big old bear hug because I knew it would be a while until I saw her again.

"Remember Tori, I will always be with you right here."

She said while pointing to my heart.

I smiled and for one last time said,

"I love you, up to the moon."

And before I woke up back in my bedroom for the last time I heard,

"And back again."

When I opened my eyes I was back in my bed and just like I was told the necklace turned into just a plain regular necklace with my name in the cross and mine and my nanny's special saying engraved on it. It was a bittersweet goodbye, but I knew she would always be with me.

I put the necklace back around my neck and got up. I threw on some clothes, went downstairs, grabbed my keys and left.

Chapter 8

I got in my car and headed to Eric's house. I knew what I had to do; I just hoped he would listen. As I pulled up to his house I noticed he wasn't home so I took off again headed to Mr. Keply's.

When I got there Mr. Keply was putting up dishes. I knocked on the door and when he saw that it was me he quickly opened the door.

"He's not here, you just missed him."

"Well, he isn't at home either. Did he say where he was going?" I asked.

"Nope, all he said was he was going somewhere to think. Tori he really does love you, he was a total mess when he came by. He told me what happened and I don't blame you."

Mr. Keply said while sitting down.

"I know that's why I need to find him. But I think I know where he might have gone."

I said while holding my necklace.

"I see you got your necklace. I take it your nanny told you everything that you needed to know, but I have to ask, did you meet my Amelia?"

I just smiled at him and grabbed his hands and wondered how he knew all at the same time.

"I did and I see where Eric gets his charm from. Now I got to go find Eric."

I said while kissing the top of Mr. Keply's baldhead after telling him that we would talk more about it later because I had a lot of questions.

I got back into my car and headed up the road to the only other place I knew Eric would go. I just hoped I wouldn't miss the turn off.

I turned off the road and looked up to see the stars shining bright like they were guiding me. As I came closer to the barn I saw Eric's truck and let out a sigh of relief. I shut off my car and the headlights and stepped out of my car. It was three in the morning and being by the water made it a little chilly.

I walked over to the truck and found it empty, so I looked around and noticed Eric sitting down by the river with a bottle of beer in his hand. Without making a sound I walked over and sat down beside him.

"It's beautiful with the moonlight shining on it."

I said.

"Tori, I'm so sorry, I never meant for you to get hurt, if I would have known that any of that was going to happen we would have never of went. You mean the world to me."

I put my finger against his lips and shushed him.

"I know, and I'm sorry I hit you without letting you explain first."

I said while laying my head down on his shoulder.

He kissed my forehead and took another sip of his beer before standing up and pulling me up with him. I wrapped my arms around his neck and kissed him. He threw his empty bottle on the back of the truck.

"I came out here to think since this is our spot."

He said while looking at the moon.

"I know, I went to your house first and you weren't there so I went to your grandpa's and he said that you had just left so I knew the only other place you would be is here."

I said while pressing into him. I saw the red mark on his face from where I slapped him and touched it softly.

"I will have to admit you do know how to hit when you get angry. Remind me never to piss you off."

Eric said jokingly.

I put my head against his head and grabbed the blanket of out his truck and headed toward the barn. I spread the blanket out on the barn floor and pulled Eric closer to me. I pulled off my shirt, threw it on the hay pile, kissed him softly and whispered in his ear, I love you Eric Keply and I want all of you.

He looked back at me with a crooked grin, picked me up and gently laid me down on the barn floor while kissing me. It felt right and so perfect, besides he knew what I wanted and I knew he wanted it too.

I woke up a few hours later with the sun beaming in through the cracks of the barn. I sat up and stretched forgetting that I was still naked. I quickly got dressed because it was freezing outside. I sat back down and kissed Eric's cheek softly waking him up. He opened his eyes and stretched.

"Dang, it's chilly out here."

He said while wrapping the blanket around him.

"I know that's I why I quickly got dressed."

I said while tossing him his clothes.

I watched him as he got dressed and helped fold the blanket after he picked it up. He kissed me softly as I got ready to get into my car to go home. I was happy that everything was okay and that if anything should ever happen again to let him explain first.

When I got home, I quickly ran upstairs to get a shower because I was chilly and I smelled like hay. I stood under the hot water for a while replaying the events that happened last night in the barn. The moment had been special and it felt so right. I stood there until the water turned cold. Once I got out I got dressed and headed down to the kitchen to start some coffee.

I sat down at my table and started to sip my coffee as I looked at the morning newspaper. Of course, there wasn't anything interesting, just the same crime and political stories. I quickly closed the paper and turned on some music. I was lost in the music when I thought I heard something hit my door. I paused the music and listened again to make sure I wasn't hearing anything. After a few moments I heard a thumping noise at my door again.

I set my coffee cup down and walked over to my door. After opening it, I looked around and didn't see anything. I shrugged my shoulders and was about to shut the door when I heard a cute little "aarf." I looked down and sitting at my door was a little fluffy solid white Pomeranian puppy. I quickly scooped her up and wondered where she had come from.

I started petting her when I noticed a piece of paper around her neck. I read the note and it read,

"Her name is Sassy, I can't keep her so whom ever finds her please take good care of her."

I smiled at this little puppy and as she licked my face I decided in that instant that she was mine now because I instantly fell in love. Later, while Eric was out helping Mr. Keply I went to the pet store and got a few things for Sassy. I started with a food and water bowl, some dog food, some cute toys and a dog bed.

Later, Eric came over for dinner. I showed him Sassy and he instantly fell in love with her too. After dinner as I cleaned up the kitchen Sassy started to play with him while he was trying to watch football. When he wasn't paying her any attention she would walk up to him and nibble on his hand. It was cute. After I got through with the dishes I went over and sat down with Eric. I loved being in his arms and near him so I asked him,

"Do you want to spend the night?"

"Do I have to sleep on the couch?"

He asked jokingly. I just looked at him with an are you serious face and headed upstairs. In just a few moments he was behind me along with Sassy. That night she slept in the bed between us. It felt like we had a kid in bed with us, which didn't bother either one of us.

As the weeks flew by Eric and I became more serious. He basically stayed every night at my house. He would go to his house occasionally to check on some things and grab some more stuff. Before I knew it, I was sharing my bathroom with some of his things, but it didn't bother me, I loved having him around. Sassy started growing like a weed and became very protective of Eric and me. She refused to sleep in her dog bed and would sleep at the foot of the bed at Eric's feet or mine. She was a very odd dog, though, because she wouldn't bark when you came through the door, she would bark and bite at your heels if you tried to leave.

Thanksgiving day finally came around and I was extremely nervous.

I would not only be spending the day with my mom, but Eric would also be meeting her. I already felt odd this thanksgiving because it was the first one without nanny and I was going to be the main one doing all the cooking. Except for the turkey, Eric was making the turkey. I was making everything else. I got up earlier than normal this morning and started the pumpkin and sweet potato pies. After I got them finished I started on the potato salad that was my nanny's recipe. She did hers a little different than most people. Her potato salad consisted of mayonnaise, pickles, onion, tomatoes and salt and pepper. I always preferred her kind over any other.

After I finished the potato salad I fixed some turkey dressing with gravy, made homemade cranberry sauce, threw together some green beans and corn and baked some butter rolls with extra butter. It was only going to be my mom, Eric, Mr. Keply and myself, but it was Thanksgiving and we were going to eat like kings and queens. Besides, we could always eat leftovers the next day.

Around 1 my mom arrived with some sweet tea and ice. She walked up, gave me a hug and a kiss and sat down.

"It smells really good in here Tori and the food looks delicious too.

So when is this Eric you speak of going to be here?"

"I think he is on his way. He texted me a few minutes ago and said that he was packing up the turkey and that he and his Grandpa would be on their way. I think you will like him, he is a real gentleman."

I said while taking a rest.

A few minutes later Eric came through the door with the turkey in his hands and Mr. Keply right behind him. He sat the turkey down in the center of the table and walked over and kissed me.

"Sorry we're late, Beauty got out of the pasture. Eric had to lure her back in with a bag of apples."

Mr. Keply said.

"I guess she wanted a thanksgiving treat too."

I said, smiling.

"Whose Beauty."

Mom asked, confused.

"Beauty is one of my very stubborn horses. You must be Tori's mom, I'm Eric's Grandpa, but you can call me Bradshaw."

Mr. Keply said.

Mom shook hands with Mr. Keply and Eric and after a few minutes of chit chat we all sat down at the table, said grace and began to dig in. Eric cut the turkey and put some on everyone's plate. He may have cooked it on the smoker, but it looked delicious and it tasted great. It was very juicy and tender, not at all dry like I feared.

I was watching everyone dig in when I saw a tear drop out of my mom's eye.

"It tastes just like hers Tori. You nailed it. Your nanny would be proud of you."

My mom saying that made my heart feel warm, so I simply smiled and began to dig in on my own plate. She was right I did nail the potato salad head on and I wasn't even trying. After we all got through eating the main meal we all sat around talking for a little bit before trying to eat any dessert because we were all full.

While mom and I were cleaning the kitchen Eric and Mr. Keply went into the living room to watch the football game that was on which was NC State against Virginia. As the game started I could hear Eric yelling at the TV.

"Eric is quite the young man, I'm impressed Tori."

"Thanks mom, he is great, I don't think I can ever imagine being without him. He really is something special."

I said.

"I have to ask though, where are his parents and why on earth is he yelling at your TV so loudly?"

She asked while putting her hands over her ears.

"His mom passed away when he was eleven and he never met his dad. Mr. Keply and Eric's grandmother raised him she passed away a couple of years ago. As far as the TV goes, he's yelling because he used to play for NC State before he hurt his knee and had to quit. He misses being able to play football."

I said, sighing.

"Ok, that explains why he is so muscular. Well, he seems like a great guy so as long as he makes you happy then I'm happy."

Mom said.

"He does he really does."

After mom and I got the kitchen clean we went in the living room to watch the game with the guys. I sat down beside Eric and asked him if he could calm down just a bit. He apologized and wrapped his arms around me. After the game mom left and soon Eric did too to take his Grandpa home. When he got back, I was already stretched out in the bed trying to read, but Sassy was having no part of that because she wanted to play. Every time I would try to read a page she would jump

on my feet or slide in-between the book and me. Finally, I threw her toy for her and she hopped down off the bed with glee.

"Sassy not letting you read again?"

Eric asked while taking off his shirt and pants and sliding into bed.

"Nope, but it's ok. How was your grandpa after you took him home?"

"He was tired, but he had a good time. We had a nice long chat on the way to his house though."

"About what?"

I asked.

"About you."

"Hmm, what about me?"

I looked at him curiously.

"Nothing bad, I promise."

Eric said with a smile.

I gave him the evil eye and smiled.

"Just promise me one thing Tori, That you will stay with me forever."

I smiled,

"I promise."

I said while kissing him softly.

Chapter 9

Fall ended and winter quickly came and since Christmas was right around the corner the bookstore traffic became extremely heavy and at times hectic. We were bringing in decent money so we didn't mind, there were even a few nights that we had to stay open later tonight being one of those nights.

"Tori honey I'll be back in a few, I have to go on an errand. I love you."

Eric said while running out the door.

I looked at Mr. Keply and he just shrugged his shoulders and went back to filling orders. Since it was Christmas time we made it to where people could place orders online and come pick them up. I was stocking books when all of a sudden I felt nauseous and sick. I stepped down off the ladder and went and took a sip of my Cheer wine hoping it would help. It didn't, I felt it coming back up so I quickly raced to the bathroom.

When I came back out Eric was back and he was excited, about what I had no idea. He looked at me and his face changed to concern.

"Tori are you ok?"

He asked.

"No, not really."

I said while running back to the bathroom.

"Babe do you need to go to the doctor?"

Eric asked.

I nodded and took a death breath.

"Yep, and I'm going right now."

I said while grabbing my keys.

I called my doctor on the way and gave her a heads up that I was on my way. I don't visit my doctor much, but when I do call her, she knows something is wrong. When I pulled into the parking lot I quickly got out of the car and headed into the office. I grabbed a barf bag incase any more came up. Thankfully, I didn't have to wait long in the waiting room. I sat waiting for maybe two minutes and was called back. I did the normal routine vital check and urine sample and went to wait in the room.

As I sat waiting I wondered what it could be going on because last week I had felt fine. As the doctor walked in she had a sheet of paper and a bag in one hand. She went over to her desk and sat down after washing her hands. I looked at her waiting for her to tell me it was a simple cold or something. She looked up at me looking very serious then as our eyes met her serious face turned into a smile. She slid the paper and the bag over to me; I glanced down and looked back up at her.

"Are you serious?"

I asked, amazed.

After being prescribed some prenatal vitamins and some nausea medicine I headed home. Once I got home, I went and sat down in the kitchen and poured me a glass of Ginger Ale to try and help me feel a little better. I was shocked by the news that I had just received, and excited at the same time. I didn't know how I was going to tell Eric but I wanted it to be in a special way. According to the doctor him or her was supposed to be here sometime around the first week of August next year.

I was daydreaming when I heard a knock on the door. I opened it to find Eric standing in front of the door with a dozen roses and a bag of chicken soup from Olive Garden. I smiled at him and took the roses from his hand as he walked in. He kissed the top of my head and sat the bag of soup on the table.

"I figured that you would be back by now and to make you feel better I brought you some soup and bread sticks from your favorite place. So what did the doctor say?"

Eric asked while getting a bowl out of the cabinet.

"Aww you're so sweet, but I'm fine, really."

I said while sitting down.

"Is it contagious?"

"No you can't catch it, but some things are fixing to change."

I said while taking a bite of soup.

He didn't seem to understand what I was trying to say instead he interrupted me.

"Speaking of change I wanted to talk with you about something, something that is going to change both of our lives."

Eric said all serious.

I just looked at him and waited to hear what he was going to say next.

"Tori, I've done some thinking and well since we are together almost all the time anyway, I thought that maybe it was time we discussed moving in together. If you want we can stay here instead of my place since yours is paid for."

I smiled and wrapped my arms around his neck while sitting down on his lap.

"I love that idea because I absolutely love you Eric and I intend on spending the rest of my life with you."

I kissed his cheek softly, got up and went back to my soup. He was right the soup did make me feel better, it eased the sick feeling and the bread sticks were even better. After we got through eating, he washed up the dishes and then cuddled with me on the couch. I ended up falling asleep in his arms again.

A couple of weeks later on the 23rd Eric and I went to the parade together. I still hadn't told him the good news and that was only because I was going to wait until Christmas morning to tell him. I did go back and see my doctor for a check up and I got to see him or her. Everything was perfect and he or she was growing right on track. I decided that I would take the picture and wrap it in a box with a cute letter.

As we watched the parade I got more and more anxious. I wanted to tell him so bad, but I also wanted to wait until Christmas morning.

He could tell I had something on my mind so he squeezed my hand and looked down at me,

"Tori is everything ok? You look like you're thinking about something."

"I am but I'm fine, you will just have to wait and see."

I said, smiling.

After the parade Eric and I decided to do some last minute Christmas shopping and get some things for Christmas dinner. Mom and Mr. Keply were joining us again like they did for Thanksgiving. I was going to tell mom the same time I told Eric. I had a feeling though that Mr. Keply already knew because at work he would look at me and smile and he wouldn't let me carry anything heavy or it could have been about whatever Eric was up to because he had been acting funny as well.

Either way we would see in a couple of days.

Mr. Keply decided to close the store early the next day and as we were closing, he had Eric run downtown to the bakery to get some cookies to give to his pigs and horses. He wanted to give his animals a Christmas present because he is that sweet of a person. A few minutes after Eric left, he asked me,

"So have you told Eric yet, or are you waiting until tomorrow?"

I looked at him and asked,

"How do you know?"

"Come on Tori, you can hide it from an old man like myself and plus your face is glowing and your wearing a dress that is one size too big."

He said while touching my shoulder.

"No, I haven't told him yet, I wanted to do it in a special way."

I said while telling him about what I had planned.

"Oh, that is going to tickle him. Boy Tori this tickles me pink knowing that I am going to be a great Grandpa. But don't worry your secret is safe with me."

He said while winking at me.

After Eric got back we told Mr. Keply good night and headed home.

It was now officially our home because Eric moved in officially last week. Sassy still doesn't know what to think about it, but she is coming around. Sassy has become my itty-bitty guard dog and is by my side where ever I go in the house.

We spent the night getting the house ready for tomorrow's festivities.

I put all the wrapped gifts under the tree except for Eric's special one.

I hid that one in my dresser because I didn't want him to become curious and open it early. We sat up until about nine watching Frosty the Snowman on TV.

"Hun, I'm tired, so I'm going to go upstairs and go to bed, are you coming?"

I asked.

"Yes, I'll be up in a few minutes I have to check on something first."

He said with a smile.

I kissed the top of his head and went on upstairs. While walking I wondered what exactly he was up to because he had been acting sneaky the past few weeks. When I got upstairs, I slid out of my dress and put on a nightgown. I looked down and noticed that I was starting to get a little bump. I touched my stomach and whispered,

"I'm going to tell your daddy about you tomorrow little one, and you just don't know how loved you are already."

I laid down and ended up falling asleep extremely easy, I guess it was because I was tired. I dreamed of nanny, she was sitting on the porch at the back of her cottage.

"Merry Christmas Tori, I love you and that baby. I know it's your first Christmas without me, but you will have your whole family around you."

I woke up to the sun shining through the window, hitting my face, I rolled over to find Eric not there so I sat up wondering where he could be. I got up out of bed and headed across the hall to the bathroom. As I looked out the bathroom window I noticed that some snow fell last night because there was some on my car. When I got done, I walked downstairs to find Eric in the kitchen. He had already made some coffee and put the ham in the oven.

"What time is it? And why didn't you wake me?"

I asked while pouring me a cup of coffee.

"You were sleeping so peacefully, I was going to let you sleep a little bit longer and bring you a special Christmas breakfast to you in bed."

"Aww, you are so sweet, I love you."

I said while kissing him softly and sitting down at the table.

Eric had made me some white chocolate pancakes and bacon. It looked and smelled so delicious. I felt like the luckiest woman in the world.

After breakfast, I walked upstairs and got dressed. I slid on a Christmas sweater and a pair of sweat pants. We decided to wait until mom and Mr. Keply got here so we could all exchange gifts at the same time. I was anxious and excited to give Eric his. I took the special gift out of my dresser and slid it under the tree in the back when I got back downstairs.

Eric and I spent the morning cooking and around noon mom and Mr. Keply showed up and they were both in a cheerful mood. Mom walked up and kissed my cheek.

"Merry Christmas baby."

She said while hugging me

I hugged her back and told her that Eric and I had decided that we would all exchange gifts together and that it would probably be after dinner.

"That's fine baby, I'm not worried. As long as I have you I'm happy."

I smiled and felt tears starting to well up in my eyes.

"Nope, none of that today."

Mom said while wiping the tear from my eye.

She didn't know it was due to my hormones so I nodded my head and went and sat down in the kitchen. Mr. Keply was sitting at the table talking with Eric who was pulling the ham out of the oven. A few minutes later everything was set on the table, we held hands and said a prayer thanking the Lord for the food when Mr. Keply added,

"And thank you for the surprises that we will be receiving in a bit."

I looked at him and he smiled a very big smile.

After we all got through eating I went into the living room and pulled out Erics special present from under the tree and went and sat back down while we went outside to talk to Mr. Keply about something.

While waiting I pulled out the eclair dessert that I had made. Mom saw and her eyes started welling up because this like the potato salad had been one of nanny's speciality dishes. I looked at her and said,

"Nope, none of that today."

We smiled and laughed together and was talking about her when Mr. Keply walked back in. I looked at him confused.

"Eric will be here in a minute, I need for you to close your eyes and keep them shut."

I smiled, wondering what was going on and simply closed my eyes.

A few moments later I heard Eric walk in.

"You can open your eyes now Tori."

I opened my eyes to find Eric holding a dozen roses in one hand and a red velvet bag in the other.

"Merry Christmas Tori."

He said while handing me the flowers. I stuck my nose down to sniff them and they smelled wonderful, when I looked back up I saw Eric pull a black box out of the red bag and drop down to one knee. At that moment I couldn't breathe and I was speechless. He opened the box and inside that box was the exact ring that I had fallen in love with at the festival. Tears started to form in my eyes, as he took my hand I heard him say,

"Tori, I love you so much, I don't want any other woman, but you, will you do me the honor of accepting my mother's ring and becoming my wife?"

"Yes, Eric Yes!

I shouted while jumping out of my chair into his arms. I kissed him softly and my mom came over and hugged us. I was wiping the tears from my eyes when I heard,

"What about your surprise for Eric Tori?"

I looked over to Mr. Keply who was smiling. I sat back down and slid the special box over to Eric while trying to hold back tears. I took a breath as he opened the box and picked up the letter. He looked and started reading out loud,

"Dear Daddy, Mommy found out about me a couple weeks ago when she went to the doctor. She wanted to make the moment special when she told you about me. I'll be here around August 5th next year and I can't wait to meet you.

I am very healthy and under this letter is a special picture of me.

Love Jr or Amelia."

As Eric finished the last line and held up the picture I saw that he was crying. He stood up and kissed me then he bent down and softly kissed my belly, which made me start crying. When he looked back up I said,

"Merry Christmas Eric."

"I'm going to be a daddy, grandpa, I'm going to be a daddy."

Eric said while hugging Mr. Keply.

"I know son, I knew before she did."

"That's true, he came to me the other day asking if I had told you yet."

Mom kissed us both and told us both congratulations and welcomed Eric to the family.

This was definitely a Christmas to remember. After we ate some eclair we opened the rest of the gifts. Eric and I got his grandpa a new flannel jacket since his other one was starting to rip. I got mom a necklace that said mom and some scented candles. Mom then handed me a bag, I opened the bag to find a big red doll. I knew instantly what the doll was, it was the Barbie doll that nanny had in her china cabinet that I had loved and wanted since I was little. I smiled and gave her a great big hug. Then Mr. Keply looked over at Eric and said,

"Son, I have a very special present for you."

Mr. Keply said while handing a bag over to Eric.

Eric opened it and I heard,

"Really grandpa? Are you sure?"

"Yes, Eric I'm sure, after your mom died your grandma and I raised you, not as our grandson but as our son. You're going to be having a baby and getting married soon and I'm getting older son. When I'm gone, I can't think of anyone else I trust more than you to run and take over my farm. So while I am still able I went ahead and signed it over to you."

Eric grabbed my hand and said,

"This truly has been a very special Christmas not only did I get to spend it with the people I love, but I also became engaged, found out I was going to be a daddy and learned that I will always have my grandpa's farm in the family. But grandpa you can't leave me any time soon. Tori, your great grandchild and I need you."

Later that evening after we all watched A Smokey Mountain Christmas and everyone left Eric and I cleaned up the kitchen. Then he picked me up and carried me up the stairs to the bedroom. He softly sat down with me in his arms and asked me,

"So my future Mrs. Keply were you serious when you put said the baby was either going to be Eric Jr or Amelia?"

"Yes, unless you think different."

I said.

"I love my mom don't get me wrong and that was sweet of you for suggesting it, but I think if its a girl we should name her after your nanny."

"Really?"

I asked.

"Yep, and if it's a boy we can name him Eric Bradshaw."

"I like that so we will either have a Sherry Lynn or an Eric Brandshaw."

I said while lying down and pulling Eric on top of me.

He didn't object and it I honestly don't think it could have been or felt even more perfect. I felt like the luckiest woman in the world.

Not only did I get my life back but I found the perfect job, my prince, a loving family and I'm getting a wonderful child and it's all thanks to my nanny and my three visits to heaven.

Chapter 10

Months went by and everything was going fantastic. The baby was growing like crazy, I was having horrible morning sickness and heartburn and Eric and I got married on May 17th at the Farm. We chose that day because it was in the spring so it wasn't too hot or too cold. Also the 17th is was my nanny's birthday and we wanted to honor her by celebrating our official union as a birthday gift to her. I wore a beautiful ivory maternity wedding gown with blue earrings and a blue necklace. Eric wore a beautiful black and blue tux. We said our vowels in the barn on hay bales in front of the horse stalls. Instead of drinking wine or champagne to celebrate we drunk Cheerwine and had a wonderful cake made by one of the bakeries up town.

It was absolutely perfect. Eric invited some of his friends from state and I invited a few of my friends that I still kept in touch with. It was a small wedding, but its what we both wanted. Mr. Keply looked very handsome at the wedding. Around January his health started to decline and he got put on oxygen. But he was determined to be in the wedding so we let him.

A few weeks after the wedding we found out that we were going to have a little girl. Eric was determined to stick with naming her after nanny, but since Sherry wasn't really a common name anymore, we decided to change the first name to Emerald so we were having an Emerald Lynn. As it came closer in time for her arrival we all became extremely excited. I ended up having to be induced because she was stubborn and didn't want to come out so after being induced Emerald made her debut appearance on August 2nd at 12:42 PM.

She was so perfect when she was born. She came out weight 8
pounds and 8 ounces. She instantly because daddy's girl. Eric was very gentle and loving with her, being a daddy fit him well.

"Honey, we made a beautiful little angel didn't we?"

Eric asked while looking at her.

"Yes, we did, I said while lying in the hospital bed."

Two days later we got released to go home and I was extremely excited. When we got home Sassy wasn't too sure about Emerald at first. She looked at her then looked back at me and back at her. Sassy over the next couple of days got used to her. Over the next two weeks Emerald grew and started to eat more. I pumped breast milk for her and she went from eating 2 ounces every four to six hours to eight ounces.

Eric and I would take turns getting up with her throughout the night, he didn't mind, he actually enjoyed it because they were bonding as he would say.

Mr. Keply absolutely loved her too. As she grew bigger though he grew weaker and I could tell it. He enjoyed showing Emerald the horses and the other animals but sadly around the middle of August Mr. Keply passed away in his sleep. I knew it was coming he told me, that night as Eric, Emerald and I were visiting he was in a great mood, he was like the Mr. Keply that I had met the year before. As we left that night he pulled me to the side as Eric went to put Emerald in the car and he said,

"Tori, it's my time I know it is. I can't say goodbye to Eric it will hurt him too much, but please promise me you will take care of him and that sweet baby for me. Let him know that I will always be with him."

"I will, but you and I both know that he for a while may not listen to me, just like I didn't listen to know one. I know that nanny sent you and Eric to me and I am very thankful. I will do everything in my power to help Eric. But he may need some help."

I said.

Mr. Keply knew what I was referring too, and winked at me. It was only a matter of hours until he went home that night. I found him because Eric had a pain hit him the moment it happened just like I felt with nanny. He didn't want to bring the baby out again so I went to check on him. Beside him was a ring and a note that said,

"Give this to Eric, you know what to do."

I took the note and stuck it in my pocket and the ring, whispered,

"I promise." and called Eric to tell him the news.

The next few days were extremely hard for Eric but Emerald and I were right by his side. We buried his Grandpa in the pasture on the farm and moved into the house. We took over the farm and the bookstore just like he wanted us to do. Weeks went by and Eric fell into the deep dark hole that I fell in but not as deep. Three weeks after his death after Emerald was asleep, he came in, he had been drinking and I decided now was the time. I told him to follow me that I had something for him.

I took him into the bedroom and gave him the ring and the note that Mr. Keply had left for him. Eric looked at me,

"This is a joke, right?"

"I assure you it's not, do you want to see?"

I asked.

At that moment Emerald woke up and my necklace started to glow, Eric just stared at me. I scooped Emerald up and took Eric's hand and led him to the closet. I opened the door and there was the same light that I saw a year ago.

"Tori, there is a light? Am I seeing things?"

"No go on in. Do you want me to go with you?"

He grabbed my hand and I led him to the door in the closet and opened it up. As the door flung open I again saw the clouds and the streets of gold. Eric was speechless and fell to his knees. As he stood back up I saw the angel that I had seen once before. She was still as beautiful as ever.

"This way Eric, What you seek is just down this path. Tori cannot go with you since she has already had her three chances."

Eric looked at me.

"Go on, give your grandpa a kiss for me, I'll be waiting for you back home."

I smiled as I watched him go and look in amazement just like I did.

I waved goodbye at the angel and in seconds I was back in the bedroom.

I fed Emerald and as she fell back asleep, I kissed her head. When Eric got back, I was reading a book.

"Do you feel better?"

I asked,

"Very, I now understand why it's called heaven. I got to see my grandpa, grandma and my mother and I got to meet Jesus."

Eric said while sitting down on the bed.

"I know, I got that same opportunity last year after my nanny died.

She's the one that led me to you. You get two more special visits Eric that only other people dream about."

I said while kissing his forehead.

"Oh, speaking of your nanny, she is a wonderful lady, and I see where you get your stubbornness from. And she told me to give you this."

He said while reaching in his pocket.

Eric handed me a note and when I opened it I read,

"Take care of that beautiful baby for me Tori, and always remember I love you up to the moon and back again."